# SHVETAKETU

IN A HERMITAGE DEEP IN THE FOREST LIVED THE LEARNED SAGE, UL... SHVETAKETU.

SHVETAKETU HAS TURNED TWELVE...

HE MUST NOW PURSUE THE STUDY OF THE SCRIPTURES.

SHVETAKETU, MY CHILD, PLEASE COME TO ME.

WHAT IS IT, FATHER?

DEAR CHILD, EVERY ONE IN OUR FAMILY HAS WITHOUT EXCEPTION, STUDIED THE SCRIPTURES AND IMBIBED THEIR MEANING.

IT IS TIME FOR YOU TOO, TO TREAD THE PATH OF LEARNING.

\* FROM CHHANDOGYA UPANISHAD.

SOON AFTERWARDS—

GO FORTH SON, AND COME BACK BRIGHT AND RESPLENDENT, WITH THE KNOWLEDGE OF THE BRAHMAN.

SHVETAKETU LEFT HIS FATHER'S HERMITAGE TO STUDY UNDER ANOTHER LEARNED RISHI.

UNDER HIS ABLE GURU, SHVETAKETU READ THE SCRIPTURES AND LEARNT THE SCIENCES; STUDIED PHILOSOPHY AND MASTERED THE ARTS.

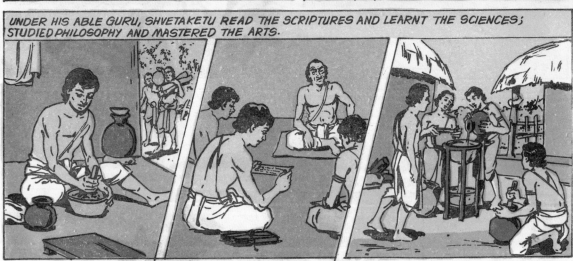

AT THE END OF TWELVE LONG YEARS, SHVETAKETU HAD LEARNT ALL THAT THERE WAS TO LEARN— AT LEAST, SO HE THOUGHT.

I HAVE NOW MASTERED NEARLY EVERYTHING THAT A MAN CAN STUDY!

PRAY, FATHER, DO TELL ME WHAT THAT KNOWLEDGE IS...

WELL SON, LOOK AT THOSE POTS AND TOYS — ALL OF THEM ARE MADE OF CLAY.

IT IS THE LUMP OF CLAY THAT, WHEN FASHIONED OUT IN A CERTAIN SHAPE, BECOMES A VESSEL, AND WHEN GIVEN ANOTHER SHAPE, BECOMES A TOY.

SO THE ESSENCE OF ALL SUCH THINGS IS CLAY. THE TOYS AND VESSELS ARE MERELY DIFFERENT NAMES GIVEN TO IT.

SO BY KNOWING A LUMP OF CLAY, ALL THAT IS MADE OF CLAY CAN BE KNOWN; BY KNOWING A NUGGET OF GOLD, ALL THAT IS MADE OF GOLD CAN BE KNOWN; AND BY KNOWING A PIECE OF IRON, ALL THAT IS MADE OF IRON CAN BE KNOWN!

THEREFORE, MY CHILD, YOU MUST GET TO KNOW THE ESSENCE OF ALL THINGS — THE ONE THING THAT EXISTS IN EVERYTHING IN THIS UNIVERSE.

I STILL DO NOT UNDERSTAND, FATHER.

THESE RIVERS, MY CHILD, PROCEED FROM THE EAST TOWARDS THE WEST, THEN FROM THE OCEAN THEY RISE IN THE FORM OF VAPOUR AND DROPPING AGAIN, MERGE INTO THE OCEAN...

JUST AS THE RIVERS DO NOT REMEMBER WHAT THEY WERE, SO ALSO ALL CREATED BEINGS DO NOT KNOW THAT THEY HAVE ISSUED FROM TRUTH.

LOOK AT THE TREE OVER THERE.

IF YOU WERE TO STRIKE AT THAT TREE, IT WOULD DISCHARGE A LITTLE SAP. PERVADED BY LIFE, IT WOULD CONTINUE TO DRAW SUSTENANCE FROM THE EARTH.

"BUT WHEN LIFE FORSAKES ONE OF ITS BRANCHES, IT DRIES UP."

EACH BRANCH FORSAKEN BY LIFE, DRIES UP.

"WHEN THE ENTIRE TREE IS FORSAKEN BY LIFE, THE WHOLE TREE DRIES UP..."

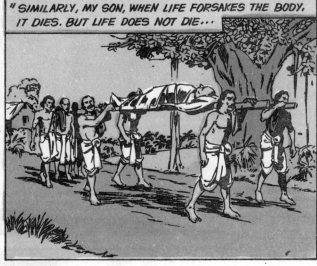

"SIMILARLY, MY SON, WHEN LIFE FORSAKES THE BODY, IT DIES. BUT LIFE DOES NOT DIE..."

...THAT WHICH DOES NOT DIE IS ATMAN. YOU ARE THAT ATMAN, WHICH IS ALL-PERVASIVE.

NOTHING FATHER.

NOTHING?

YES, NOTHING!

IF THERE IS NOTHING IN THE SEED, HOW CAN THAT NOTHING GIVE RISE TO A MIGHTY BANYAN TREE?

THEN WHAT IS THAT "SOMETHING" WHICH WE CANNOT SEE, FATHER?

THAT, SHVETAKETU, IS THE ESSENCE OF ALL THINGS—THE ATMAN—THAT PERVADES THE UNIVERSE, YOU TOO ARE THAT, O SHVETAKETU!

—AND IF WE CANNOT SEE THE ESSENCE, HOW DO WE KNOW THAT IT EXISTS?

I SHALL EXPLAIN TO YOU. PUT THIS SALT IN WATER.

SHVETAKETU DID AS HE WAS TOLD—

HERE IS THE POT OF WATER WITH SALT IN IT, FATHER.

KEEP IT ASIDE FOR NOW. BRING IT TO ME TOMORROW MORNING.

EARLY THE NEXT MORNING, SHVETAKETU WENT TO HIS FATHER WITH THE POT—

CAN YOU SEE THE SALT YOU PUT INTO THIS POT LAST EVENING, SHVETAKETU?

THE SALT HAD DISSOLVED.

NO FATHER, I CANNOT.

NOW TASTE THE WATER AT THE TOP OF THE POT, SHVETAKETU. HOW IS IT?

MM... IT'S SALTY.

NOW TASTE FROM THE MIDDLE OF THE POT.

SHVETAKETU DIPPED A FINGER IN THE MIDDLE OF THE POT AND TASTED THE WATER.

IT'S SALTY AGAIN, FATHER.

AND NOW TASTE THE WATER AT THE BOTTOM.

IT STILL IS SALTY FATHER.

NOW LOOK AGAIN FOR THE SALT YOU PUT IN IT YESTERDAY.

10

# RAIKVA THE CARTMAN*

JANASHRUTI, THE KING OF MAHAVRASHA WAS A BENEVOLENT AND GENEROUS RULER.

HE BUILT REST HOUSES ALONG THE ROADS OF HIS KINGDOM, WHERE FREE FOOD AND LODGING WERE PROVIDED TO TRAVELLERS.

HE ALSO BUILT HOSPITALS AND HOMES TO CARE FOR THE SICK, THE NEEDY AND THE AGEING.

\* FROM CHHANDOGYA UPANISHAD.

...AND HE TAXED HIS SUBJECTS FAIRLY. QUITE NATURALLY JANASHRUTI WAS PLEASED WITH HIMSELF FOR HAVING DONE SO MUCH FOR HIS KINGDOM.

GLORY TO KING JANASHRUTI.

HIS FAME SPREAD FAR BEYOND THE BORDERS OF MAHAVRASHA. UNFORTUNATELY IT DID NOT TAKE LONG TO TURN HIM INTO A VAIN MAN.

AH! IT IS I WHO AM PROVIDING FOOD TO ALL THESE PEOPLE. HOW MUCH MERIT I HAVE EARNED. THE DEVAS TOO MUST BE PLEASED WITH ME...

ONE EVENING WHILE HE WAS RELAXING ON THE TERRACE OF HIS PALACE—

SUCH LOVELY SWANS!

JANASHRUTI FELT RESTLESS THAT NIGHT.

RAIKVA! I MUST SEND MY MEN TOMORROW TO FIND OUT WHO THIS RAIKVA IS, WHERE HE IS...

EARLY THE NEXT MORNING, THE ELABORATE RITUAL TO WAKE UP THE ROYAL PERSONAGE BEGAN—

WAKE UP, O SAVIOUR OF THE MASSES!

ARISE, O PROVIDER OF THE MILLIONS!!

ARISE O CELESTIAL AMONG MEN!

STOP! STOP ALL THIS FALSE PRAISE!

YOU SHALL STOP PRAISING ME THUS FOR I AM NOT WORTHY OF SUCH PRAISE!

WHAT IS IT, MAHARAJ? WHAT BOTHERS OUR BENEVOLENT KING?

WHAT DOES OUR WORTHY KING SEEK FROM AN ORDINARY MAN LIKE HIM.

JANASHRUTI'S DELIGHT KNEW NO BOUNDS WHEN HE WAS TOLD THAT RAIKVA HAD FINALLY BEEN FOUND.

MAKE PREPARATIONS TO LEAVE IMMEDIATELY FOR RAIKVA'S VILLAGE.

NEXT MORNING, JANASHRUTI STARTED FOR RAIKVA'S VILLAGE WITH AN ENTOURAGE OF HIS MEN. HE TOOK WITH HIM AN IMPRESSIVE ARRAY OF 600 COWS, A GOLD NECKLACE AND A CARRIAGE AS A GIFT TO RAIKVA.

ARRIVING AT THE VILLAGE, JANASHRUTI INTRODUCED HIMSELF.——

I HAVE HEARD OF YOU AS ONE WHO HAS EARNED GREAT MERIT, ONE WHO HAS LEARNT ALL THERE IS TO LEARN AND ONE WHO KNOWS BRAHMAN.

O WISE RAIKVA, I SHALL PRESENT YOU WITH 600 COWS, THIS SPLENDID NECKLACE AND THIS CARRIAGE AND WHATEVER ELSE THAT YOU DESIRE.

PLEASE IMPART TO ME THE SUPREME KNOWLEDGE OF BRAHMAN...

O IGNORANT KING! THE KNOWLEDGE OF BRAHMAN CANNOT BE PURCHASED.

KNOWLEDGE IS NOT A COMMODITY. IT CANNOT BE BARTERED, BEGONE O JANASHRUTI. YOU ARE NOT YET READY TO RECEIVE THE SUPREME KNOWLEDGE.

A DISAPPOINTED JANASHRUTI MADE HIS WAY BACK TO THE KINGDOM, AT ONCE SAD AND HUMBLED.

AFTER A FEW WEEKS, WHEN HE HAD DEEPLY PONDERED OVER HIS MEETING WITH RAIKVA, HE MADE PREPARATIONS TO MEET RAIKVA AGAIN.

I WONDER HOW I CAN CONVINCE HIM THAT I AM REALLY KEEN TO RECEIVE THE KNOWLEDGE OF THE BRAHMAN.

ONCE AGAIN HE SET OUT WITH HIS LARGE ENTOURAGE. THIS TIME HIS BEAUTIFUL DAUGHTER ACCOMPANIED HIM.

ON REACHING THE VILLAGE, HE PROSTRATED BEFORE THE WISE RUSTIC.

O WISE RAIKVA, LAST TIME I CAME TO YOU AS A KING...

...BUT I HAVE SHED MY ROYAL EGO, AND I SURRENDER MYSELF TO YOU...

THIS TIME, RAIKVA SAW THAT THE KING HAD LOST ALL HIS VANITY AND THE GENUINE DESIRE FOR KNOWLEDGE WAS EVIDENT FROM HIS EYES.

I BLESS YOU, O VIRTUOUS JANASHRUTI. ALL THE KNOWLEDGE THAT IS MINE SHALL NOW BE YOURS.

AND THEN RAIKVA, DRAWING JANASHRUTI CLOSE TO HIM, SPOKE AT LENGTH —

THE SUPREME KNOWLEDGE CANNOT BE IMBIBED UNLESS ONE HAS SHED ONE'S EGO.

ONLY THE HUMBLE CAN PERCEIVE THE BRAHMAN.

NOW THAT YOU ARE HUMBLE, I WILL INSTRUCT YOU ABOUT THE SUPREME KNOWLEDGE.

AND SO SAYING RAIKVA ACCEPTED JANASHRUTI AS HIS DISCIPLE.

# WHEN THE DEVAS WERE HUMBLED*

THIS STORY WAS TOLD BY AN ANCIENT RISHI TO HIS DISCIPLES TO ILLUSTRATE HOW BRAHMAN, THE SELF-EXISTING, ALL-PERVADING POWER, RESTORES ORDER IN THE WORLD WHENEVER EVIL AND DISORDER SEEM TO PLAGUE IT.

LONG AGO, THE DEVAS HAD A WAR WITH THE ASURAS* YOU KNOW, AS IT USUALLY HAPPENS THE GOOD LACK STRENGTH AND THE STRONG LACK GOODNESS...

"... AFTER DAYS OF FIERCE FIGHTING, IT SEEMED THAT THE ASURAS WERE GETTING THE UPPER HAND FOR THEY WERE STRONG, UNPRINCIPLED AND RUTHLESS ..."

...AND WHEN THE DEVAS BEGAN TO LOSE HEAVILY, A FEW OF THEM PRAYED TO BRAHMAN TO COME TO THEIR AID."

O BRAHMAN, IF YOU DO NOT HELP US IN THIS WAR, ONLY EVIL AND DISORDER SHALL RULE THIS EARTH. COME TO OUR AID, O DIVINE FATHER.

GO FORTH AND FIGHT WITH ALL YOUR MIGHT. ONLY GOOD CAN TRIUMPH IN THE END.

"INVIGORATED BY THIS DIVINE ASSURANCE, THE DEVAS FOUGHT BACK BRAVELY...

"...AND WITH DIVINE HELP, IT DID NOT TAKE THEM LONG TO VANQUISH THE ASURAS.

"OVERJOYED WITH THEIR VICTORY THE DEVAS CELEBRATED WITH GAY ABANDON.

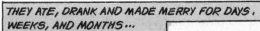

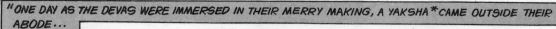

"ONE DAY AS THE DEVAS WERE IMMERSED IN THEIR MERRY MAKING, A YAKSHA* CAME OUTSIDE THEIR ABODE...

"THE YAKSHA SOON CAUGHT INDRA'S EYE.

GO AND FIND OUT WHO THIS BEING IS AND WHAT BRINGS HIM HERE, O AGNI.

"AGNI APPROACHED THE YAKSHA AND SPOKE FIRST —

I AM AGNI, THE LORD OF FIRE...

"BEFORE AGNI COULD FINISH HIS SENTENCE, THE YAKSHA ASKED HIM A QUESTION —

O AGNI, LORD OF FIRE, WHAT GREAT POWERS DO YOU POSSESS?

I CAN BURN AND DESTROY ANYTHING THAT EXISTS.

✳ DIVINE BEING

THEN PLEASE COME FORWARD AND BURN THIS BLADE OF GRASS—REDUCE IT TO ASHES.

WHAT? THIS MERE BLADE OF GRASS? HO HO HA HA.

YES, PLEASE BURN THIS BLADE OF GRASS.

"...AND AGNI WITH HIS MIGHTY POWERS ORDERED THE FIRE TO BURN UP THAT BLADE OF GRASS...

AGNI RAGED AND THE FLAMES ENGULFED THE BLADE OF GRASS BUT NO MATTER HOW HARD HE TRIED, HE COULD NOT SUCCEED—

UH!

" AFTER HAVING FAILED TO INCINERATE THAT SINGLE BLADE, HE WALKED BACK TO THE PALACE DEJECTED AND HUMBLED. HE WONDERED WHO THIS STRANGE POWERFUL BEING WAS.

"VAYU TOO WENT BACK TO THE PALACE THE WAY AGNI HAD — FATIGUED AND HUMBLED BUT NOT REALISING WHO THE YAKSHA WAS.

... AND THEN INDRA HIMSELF STEPPED OUT—

"SUDDENLY THE YAKSHA DISAPPEARED.

?

"INDRA LOOKED HERE AND THERE FOR THE YAKSHA BUT COULD NOT FIND HIM. INSTEAD HIS EYES FELL UPON UMA, THE GODDESS OF SPIRITUAL KNOWLEDGE, WHO HAPPENED TO PASS BY...

UMA!

HE APPEARED THUS IN FRONT OF YOU ONLY TO BRING YOU BACK TO YOUR SENSES, O DEVAS.

YOU HAVE HAD ENOUGH OF CELEBRATIONS OF YOUR VICTORY. IT IS NOW TIME TO GET BACK TO THE ONEROUS DUTIES OF RULING.

"REALISING THEIR FOLLY, THE DEVAS SETTLED DOWN TO A MORE SENSIBLE LIFE..."

AND THUS BRAHMAN HAD ONCE AGAIN BROUGHT ORDER AND METHOD INTO THE WORLD.

# THE BOLD BEGGAR*

SHAUNAKA KAPEYA AND ABHIPRATARIN KAKSHASENI WERE TWO SAGES WHO LIVED IN A HERMITAGE IN THE FOREST. THEY SPENT MOST OF THEIR TIME WORSHIPPING VAYU, THE GOD OF WIND.

ONE AFTERNOON, AS THE SAGES WERE TO BEGIN THEIR MEAL···

···A BRAHMACHARI ARRIVED WITH HIS BOWL.

NO, MY BOY, WE CANNOT SPARE YOU ANY FOOD.

*FROM CHHANDOGYA UPANISHAD.

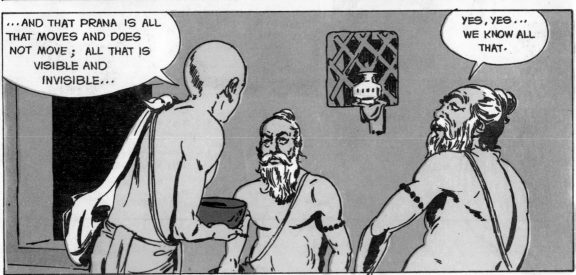

IF PRANA PERVADES THE UNIVERSE, IT PERVADES ME TOO. WHO AM I BUT A PART OF THE UNIVERSE... AM I NOT?

UH.... YES, YOU ARE.

IT IS PRANA THAT PULSATES IN ME, AS THIS HUNGRY BODY OF MINE STANDS BEFORE YOU AND SPEAKS...

YOU SPEAK THE TRUTH, O YOUNG BRAHMANA!

THEN O REVERED RISHIS, IN DENYING ME FOOD, YOU ARE DENYING PRANA FOR WHOM YOU HAVE PREPARED THE FOOD.

AND THE SAGES, WHO SO FAR HAD ONLY UNDERSTOOD THE LITERAL MEANING OF THE SCRIPTURES, REALISED THEN THE SPIRIT BEHIND THE WORDS. ASHAMED AT THEIR IGNORANCE, THEY GLADLY SHARED THEIR FOOD WITH THE YOUNG BRAHMANA!

# RE-INTRODUCING AMAR CHITRA KATHA SUBSCRIPTIONS!!

# SUBSCRIBE NOW

## SUBSCRIBER DETAILS

Name _____

Date of Birth _____

Address _____

_____

City _____ Pin _____

State/Country _____

Phone _____

Email _____

Signature _____

☐ I have subscribed earlier to ACK/Tinkle.
(Please tick)

## SUBSCRIPTION PLAN

**TINKLE Magazine**
☐ 1 Year
☐ 2 Years
☐ 3 Years

**TINKLE Digest**
☐ 1 Year
☐ 2 Years
☐ 3 Years

**COMBO Subscription**
☐ 1 Year
☐ 2 Years
☐ 3 Years

## PAYMENT OPTIONS

☐ Pay by Money Order

☐ Pay by Cheque/DD
a) Enclosed cheque/DD in favour of
'Amar Chitra Katha Pvt. Ltd.'
b) Please add Rs. 15 for Non-Mumbai cheques

☐ Pay by credit card
a) Card type: ☐ Visa ☐ Master
b) Please charge Rs. _____ to my
credit card number _____
c) Expiry date _____
d) Card member's signature _____

☐ Pay by VPP (Value Payable Post) – Pay cash
on delivery of 1st issue to the postman
(Additional charges of Rs. 24)

Mail to: Amar Chitra Katha Pvt. Ltd. 14, Marthanda,
84, Dr. Annie Besant Road, Worli, Mumbai – 400 018.
Tel.: 022-6629 6999/838 Fax: 022-6629 6900
Email: tinklesubscription@ack-media.com
SMS: ACK BUY to 575758

---

**Subscribers receive their copies before the newsstands!!**

### TINKLE Magazine
72 pages of new stories every month!

|  | Stand Price | India | Overseas |
|---|---|---|---|
| 1 Year | Rs. 240 | Rs. 225 | Rs. 112 |
| 2 Years | Rs. 480 | Rs. 440 | Rs. 202 |
| 3 Years | Rs. 720 | Rs. 640 | Rs. 292 |

### TINKLE Digest
96 pages of the best stories from the past issues of Tinkle magazine!

|  | Stand Price | India | Overseas |
|---|---|---|---|
| 1 Year | Rs. 480 | Rs. 450 | Rs. 157 |
| 2 Years | Rs. 960 | Rs. 880 | Rs. 292 |
| 3 Years | Rs. 1440 | Rs. 1280 | Rs. 405 |

### COMBO Subscription
Best of both new and old Tinkle!*

|  | Stand Price | India | Overseas |
|---|---|---|---|
| 1 Year | Rs. 720 | Rs. 640 | Rs. 225 |
| 2 Years | Rs. 1440 | Rs. 1260 | Rs. 427 |
| 3 Years | Rs. 2160 | Rs. 1830 | Rs. 607 |

* Tinkle magazine and digest arrive separately.

---

**You can also subscribe at www.tinkleonline.com. Tinkleonline users get upto 1750 bonus Tinkle Gold coins on subscribing online!**